THIS OLD MAN

ILLUSTRATED BY CAROL JONES

Houghton Mifflin Company

Walter Lorraine  Books

Copyright © 1990 by Carol Jones

ISBN 0-395-54699-0 (cl.).   ISBN 0-395-90124-3 (pbk.).

LC: 90-35332

First American edition 1990 by Houghton Mifflin Company

Originally published in Australia in 1990 by Angus&Robertson
now an imprint of HarperCollins*Publishers* Pty Limited
http://www.harpercollins.com.au

Printed in Hong Kong

10 9 8 7

For Sally and Mark

This old man he played . . .

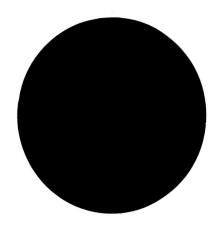

ONE

He played nick nack on my . . .

DRUM

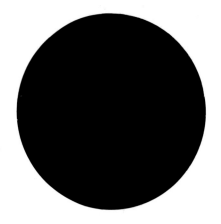

With a nick nack Paddy whack,

give a dog a bone.

This old man came rolling home.

This old man he played . . .

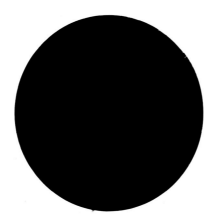

TWO

He played nick nack on my . . .

SHOE

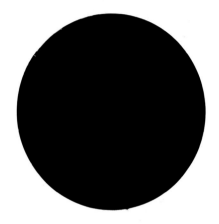

With a nick nack Paddy whack,

give a dog a bone.

This old man came rolling home.

This old man he played . . .

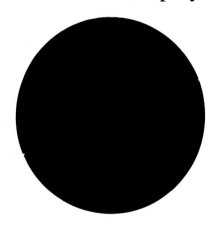

THREE

He played nick nack on my . . .

KNEE

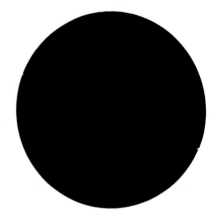

With a nick nack Paddy whack,

give a dog a bone.

This old man came rolling home.

This old man he played . . .

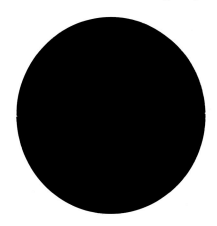

FOUR

He played nick nack on my . . .

DOOR

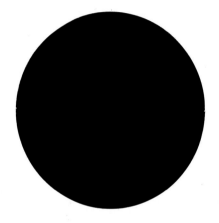

With a nick nack Paddy whack,

give a dog a bone.

This old man came rolling home.

This old man he played . . .

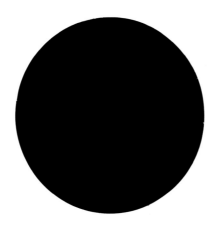

FIVE

He played nick nack on my . . .

HIVE

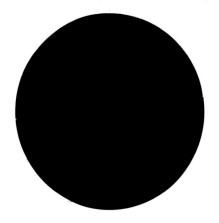

With a nick nack Paddy whack,

give a dog a bone.

This old man came rolling home.

This old man he played . . .

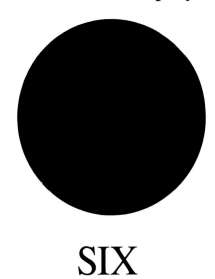

SIX

He played nick nack on my . . .

STICKS

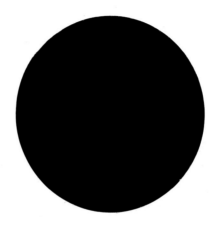

With a nick nack Paddy whack,

give a dog a bone.

This old man came rolling home.

This old man he played . . .

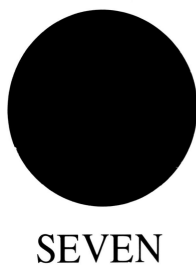

SEVEN

He played nick nack up to . . .

HEAVEN

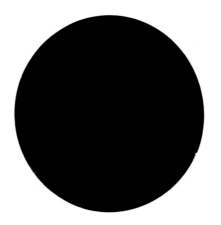

With a nick nack Paddy whack,

give a dog a bone.

This old man came rolling home.

This old man he played . . .

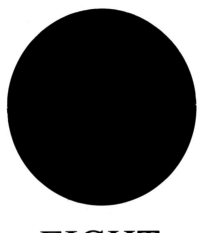

EIGHT

He played nick nack on my . . .

GATE

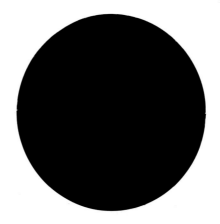

With a nick nack Paddy whack,

give a dog a bone.

This old man came rolling home.

This old man he played . . .

NINE

He played nick nack on my . . .

LINE

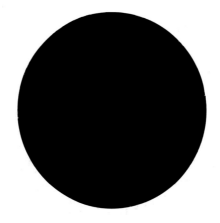

With a nick nack Paddy whack,

give a dog a bone.

This old man came rolling home.

This old man he played . . .

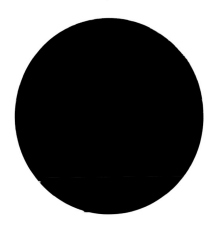

TEN

He played nick nack on my . . .

HEN

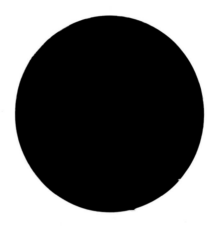

With a nick nack Paddy whack,

give a dog a bone.

This old man came rolling home.

THIS OLD MAN

This arrangement © John Aué 1990

This old man,
He played ONE,
He played nick nack on my DRUM.
Chorus:
With a nick nack Paddy whack,
Give a dog a bone,
This old man came rolling home.

This old man,
He played TWO,
He played nick nack on my SHOE.
Chorus

This old man,
He played THREE,
He played nick nack on my KNEE.
Chorus

This old man,
He played FOUR,
He played nick nack on my DOOR.
Chorus

This old man,
He played FIVE,
He played nick nack on my HIVE.
Chorus

This old man,
He played SIX,
He played nick nack on my STICKS.
Chorus

This old man,
He played SEVEN,
He played nick nack up to HEAVEN.
Chorus

This old man,
He played EIGHT,
He played nick nack on my GATE.
Chorus

This old man,
He played NINE,
He played nick nack on my LINE.
Chorus

This old man,
He played TEN,
He played nick nack on my HEN.
Chorus